THE SHAPES OF A1R
QU4NTUM FICT10N

GABRIELA A. ARCINIEGAS

Illustrated by Ana Parker
Translation coordinated by
Dr. Raelynne M. Hale, PhD.

CALIFORNIA STATE UNIVERSITY
FULLERTON

Original Title: "Las formas del aire, ficción cuántica"
Author: Gabriela A. Arciniegas© @arciniegaslibros
Editorial services: Cuatro Ojos Editorial
Spanish edition: Bogotá, Colombia, 2019
ISBN 978-958-48-7539-6

THE SHAPES OF A1R QU4NTUM FICT10N is a collaborative project coordinated by Dr. Raelynne M. Hale at the Department of Modern Languages and Literatures, California State University, Fullerton.
English version: Osorno, Chile, 2022
ISBN 978-958-49-5206-6
Cover design and illustrations:
Ana Parker© @andromedaexplorer
Layout by: Gabriela A. Arciniegas©

Translation by:

Wendy Acosta
Monica Alonso
Isabell Chavez-Munguia
Jocelyn Contreras
Rebeca De La Cruz
Ian Finley
T. Logan Harrison
Brenda Heredia

Ezequiel Mata Jr.
Dolores A. Melchor
Alejandro Murillo
Karen Ortega
Priscilla Ortiz
Kimberly Rodriguez
Paola Ruiz Becerra
Kimberly D. Solis

CONTENTS

THANKS TO 7
PROLOGUE 9
ASÍ LO SOÑÓ 11
VASE 14
BULLS 17
THE SINGING SORCERESS 18
A NON-EUCLIDEAN REALITY.............................21
THE FOOT 29
TWENTY ARMS 34
The projector stopped working.............................35
MAX 37
No, it wasn't the skipping of a heartbeat,.............................40
SEED 43
THE LAST NIGHT 45
THE SHAPES OF AIR 46
ARIADNE 47
THE DRAGONFLY AND TIME.............................53
LEIBNIZ AND ARCHIMEDES.............................54
SLAUGHTER 55
DO NOT STOP 57
NORMA 58
CLOUDS 60
THE STUDY OF CÉZANNE'S STUDY OF MONT SAINT-VICTOIRE 62

SCHRÖDINGER'S BATHERS 64
THE FOREIGN WOMAN 65
A FIRE'S FABLE 67
APHID 69
SUNROOTS 70
PLANCK TIME 73
THE TRIUMPH OF WATER 76
THE BEGINNING: THE CHICKEN OR THE EGG?80
A DIALOGUE WITH "PLANCK TIME"................82

THANKS TO

Dr. Raelynne M. Hale, coordinator of this project as part of the course SPAN 471, Practice in Translation I. The Department of Modern Languages and Literatures at California State University, Fullerton. And special thanks to all the students who participated in this project with all their sweat and tears:

Wendy Acosta
Monica Alonso
Isabell Chavez-Munguia
Jocelyn Contreras
Rebeca De La Cruz
Ian Finley
T. Logan Harrison
Brenda Heredia

Ezequiel Mata Jr.
Dolores A. Melchor
Alejandro Murillo
Karen Ortega
Priscilla Ortiz
Kimberly Rodriguez
Paola Ruiz Becerra
Kimberly D. Solis

PROLOGUE

One of the many tasks of a translator is to work intimately with a literary piece, transforming it from one language to another, while maintaining its beauty, structure, and essence. The task can be extremely challenging, especially for those unfamiliar with the nuances of literary translation. The students in SPAN 471, Practice in Translation I, a course offered in the Certificate in Translation: Spanish to English / English to Spanish program at California State University, Fullerton, spent the entire semester diving deep into Gabriela A. Arciniegas' short story collection *Las formas del aire: ficción cuántica*. Students worked individually and in small groups to create this lovely translation, *The Shapes of Air: Quantum Fiction*, and in the process, found themselves transformed. Throughout the semester, students got to know Arciniegas and her work. She generously offered weeks of her time to meet with students, answer their questions, and help them find their voices and confidence as translators. Each student came eager to learn and ready to work hard, editing and refining draft after draft over the course of 10 weeks. What lies ahead of these pages is not only an exploration of Arciniegas' work in English, but the product of a new generation of excellent translators. Arciniegas and I would often joke that we made the perfect team, with her expertise in Spanish, short story writing, and a flare for the creative, and my expertise in English, eye for detail, and love of *cuentos*. We could not be more proud of the hard work of the students in SPAN 471 this Fall 2021 semester.

Dr. Raelynne M. Hale
Fullerton, California, 2021

ASÍ LO SOÑÓ

Translated by Brenda Heredia

She found herself sitting on a bed staring at the opened door. Was it hers? It could not be, her bedroom was, had been, warm, comfortable. This one made her think of dry, wilted leaves. Some of the geometric shapes around her were familiar, like the oval-shaped mirror in the closet, and the long rectangular shape of the bed. The light from the window began to fade as it hit the hallway wall. But it seemed like it came to life suddenly, more yellow and bright from another door in front of her, each time feeling closer with each step. For a moment, she felt her body was a painful thing that carried her. She felt like she was floating. She even thought she was dead.

She finally found out the light in front of her came from a kitchen. How had she not seen something like that so close to her room? Was it coming from her own space? Where did it come from? How would she get back?

The kitchen spread all the way to her right, it was dirty, neglected. That was not how I took care of it, she thought to herself, this cannot be my kitchen, everything looks so old, so sad. The people living there seemed so careless. The people... I remember I had a son... The kitchen. The what? The room, full of junk. Yes... full of thi-- tho-- colors flooded with yellow. For some reason her eyes had to be there. There was a vague harmony in the image. And then she saw her. A girl. Who turned around and smiled at her. Did they know each other? The girl looked friendly. She felt sorry, she was going to apologize for being there, so far from home. But then the girl said a name. At first it seemed like a name. It was a name she liked, a name that had been... maybe it was just that she liked the name. The name... faded into sounds, fragments of a song, and she tried to sing it. Among increasingly imprecise and blurry shapes in the room, something else moved, just behind that kind stranger, looking at her with those eyes so similar to her son's, which were her own... the man, round, smiled at her, but those eyes, that made her feel love, looked at her so sad and tired. The couple was looking at her and they were hugging each other like two cells, while staring at a pot on the stove, as if they were before a blue flame god. She knew about the divinity of fire because she was also drawn to the heat and the slight crackle of the flame. She managed to start a prayer, and then she acknowledged the greedy shadow that slowly took over her and her memories. Then, that warming blue substance looked meaningless to her. What a strange piece of furniture where they have the pot, she thought. She looked back into the man's eyes, who are you, who are you, she wondered, failing to find the words to form the question. She craved for the answer but she remembered that she had not known it for a long time. She knew that she loved him, she knew that he had made her cry, have you seen my son, she wanted to ask, but the question was behind glass, she could see the words, but not understand them. Could this be a dream? How long until she could wake up? She froze, she just kept staring at them. Neither the man nor the woman looked at her, the woman just kept stirring the pot while the man started swinging his body and the body of the beloved one in a silent dance. She started feeling like she did not exist, like she was merely a mind without a body, that she could only watch them. Even more, the air that separated her from that scene was solidifying, it became a sheet of glass. And suddenly, it hit her. The only possible language was: Where am I? Who are these people? She did not know. Maybe she did not know if they were even human. Did she ever know? There was no past. Just that terrifying moment of not knowing, of not understanding. And almost at the same time, when he looked at her, she felt threatened even though she couldn't understand his gesture, when the man ordered her: "go to bed." "To bed?," she searched for the sounds, her soul made an exhausting effort while connecting the words. "Your bed," the man said. Ah, yes, my bed, my bed.

VASE

Translated by Brenda Heredia

The soul is engraved, chiseled on the body. If I had not had this miserable life, I would be a different person. A vase's value does not depend on itself but on its design. The design is what invokes the emptiness that will be given to the vase. Being full is just a temporary state of the vase. The vase was not created to be filled, but to contain emptiness. Emptiness is the main aspiration of the vase and it is the kind of emptiness that determines its value. When I was little, I wanted to be a beautiful vase. Wanting beauty is a part of human nature. It is the only way to be. So I let life sculpt me, with its axes and knives. Beauty is nothing but a way of tiredness and permanent pain. I would love to know when the engraving is over and when I shall begin to die. Do we start dying once we understand beauty? Once we understand the inscription engraved on our souls?

BULLS

Translated by Brenda Heredia

If only it were about watching them run. I wish it were only about allowing them to run through the fields contemplating their magnificence, admiring their tensed muscles under their lustrous skin, trapped yet free. I wish it were only about looking at them as they get closer, and seeing the blue reflection of the sky in the dark lakes of their pupils. If it were only enough to capture the violence of their hooves tearing up the dirt, their colossal matter brushing against the air, the perfectness of the wind like a bullfighter teasing their soft horns, horns that would be the envy of Fibonacci and Vitruvius. What if the helicoids of their joyous twirls were good enough to be called art? What if going to the bullfights was just about watching them run through the fields, watching them falling in love and playing like bulls with their cows and their calves? Or watching them battle, horn against horn, like magnificent Titans. If it were possible to, maybe, allow them to watch us, in our vulnerability, allow them to smell our carnivorous breath, from the other side of the fence, without fear?

THE SINGING SORCERESS

Translated by Ezequiel Mata Jr.

Angels surround the Great Roldana. On sleepless nights, they surround her each time she dares to escape the world, instead of using her eyes to see, she uses them to hear. Colored voices come rushing to her like a stampede in water. They told her once, that "your life is a seven-headed Hydra." That's why she bathes in the blood of the dragon and the tears of her watering eyes. The size of the dragon is such that it's hard to find his head among all those scales and muscles. Each day I am presented with a dragon's scale and pounding tide of his internal bloodstreams. Each day I feel the dragon and all the faces staring at me and the voices to which I reply with platitudes are part of the dragon. Meanwhile, the higher I get the less I can see his head.

Not too long ago, I was told "to sit at the top of his head you must leap over three of his wings: earth, water and fire. The water will slowly mold the pebbles of your soul, but don't you try to hold it in your hands for it will keep pouring back into its winding course. You must drink the water to recall other names you've had. But beware of it because after a while you will find that water tasteless, and your mouth will long for something different. The earth will sculpt your earth, blow by blow and it will rip your eyes and your mouth until they open. The fire will become two; the fire at the core of your earth will turn it into a clay-burning oven; and the fire that covers your valleys and hills will transform you, mold you into a star, a meteorite."

And now two whirlwinds inside me keep spinning in opposite directions, each time someone gets near me, I wake up. And like two neighboring gears we move as a rhythmic clock and when our gaze connects through our invisible eyes I see their journey. I know how many times they have cried before this day; I know if they have not been truthful or have not yet asked for forgiveness from the same clock that moves us, and I see their untaken path and the answers they are still searching for. I do not speak to them. My mission is to remain in the shadows. I made a vow of silence, and my objective is to speak by moving the boundaries of their life, to change their path and guide them unseen. That's the lesson I have learned from the angels.

This and their songs.

The Great Roldana, singing sorceress, releases a powerful scream of silence. At the magnanimous podium of the Gods, she pauses to sing, receiving applause and a standing ovation. She sings what mankind has forgotten.

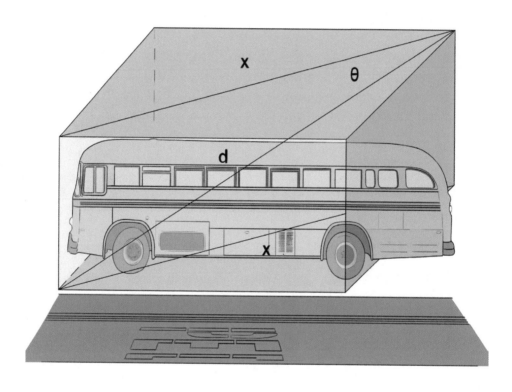

A NON-EUCLIDEAN REALITY

*Translated by Wendy Acosta
and Paola Ruiz Becerra*

I. HYPNOS

Luis Guillermo is the man of my dreams. I once met a Luis Guillermo, but he wasn't the one of my dreams; the one of my dreams I still haven't met. He doesn't live on this side, he lives in the non-Euclidean reality of dreams, but the Euclidean reality does not exist on this side either. The reality of proportions and perspective is an aberration. The non-Euclidean is everywhere and if we lower our guard, the chunks of reality messily pile up in our brain which is like the eyes of a fly. I'm sitting on the bus unable to fit my legs within my spot. The leg of a stranger brushes up against mine each time the bus accelerates or brakes. Accelerates or brakes. Brakes as in refrains, as in refraining a frantic state. The trees outside never seem to stay still. They pass by disheveled in a neverending line and crying about who-knows-what. The streetlights on one side, whereas the trees on the other. The corner of a bag sticking onto the crotch of a padded jean that pushes, forcing its way towards the back of the bus. A butt is smashed against my shoulder. A phone rings. It has rung three times already with the same ringtone, but the woman who answers has used a different tone. The *bringg bringg* mutates every time she answers. It manifests itself in different forms like the burning bush, the voice from the sky and the parted sea. I thought about the call that I answered in front of all those messy and uneven eyes that would look at me and those ears that imperceptibly rotated toward me like tiny satellite antennas. I remember the sound of his voice, the noise of the street and the breeze blowing, the promise of a coffee, the man who introduced us. I smile for no one because no one is looking at me. The bulky bag brushes past my ear, but yes, yes, a pair of eyes is looking at me. At me? Whom? For which of these bodies asymmetrically crowded, reproduced, doing meiosis in that matrix?

Every minute there are more of us. Every minute the driver receives another $0.38 in the metal box. Every minute the surface of the window receives less heat from one side and more heat on the other. The mirrored glass curves one nanometer more, in some places towards us and in others away from us. Beside the woman answering the call from the same ringtone, we all stay quiet.

However, there is still noise. The buzzing from the overlapping thoughts of everyone, the grunting of all our bowels in motion, the bubbling of all the chemical reactions produced by the mixing of ingredients from lunch and coffee. Sealed alembics, each with a slightly different design. A fractal made up of diverse elements. Yes, I know that isn't a fractal, but what is? The wheels are round, and we are inside a *paralelepípedo*[1] with windows and seats theoretically repeated, however none of that is really so.

The bus bounces and we remain unevenly suspended for a couple of seconds in the void. For a couple of seconds, gravity stops playing. If I close my eyes, I will feel my hands coming out of my face, my knee against my cheek, my butt over the crown of my head. I forget the number of my limbs, the sum of my teeth, and the length of the strands of my hair. I wake up, someone's thigh presses my scapula each time the bus jumps and the gravity stops for a second.

---

1 Parallelepiped, a geometrical shape in the form of rectangular parallel lines.

The man of my dreams will always have a different face. I recognize him by a *je ne sais quoi*. Each time I close my eyes, I am given a distinct nationality, a different native tongue, and an X age. Sometimes he recognizes me, sometimes he doesn't and then I wake up mourning. Every time someone gets on that bus, they always have a different face and a different skin tone and hand out money in bills and coins of different amounts. The only thing is that the result of the sum is either $0.38 a day or $0.40 a night. Neither 3-dollar bills nor rupees will be accepted. The driver is the only one whose face remains the same, but I only see ¼ of it, that is, the ear, the tip of the nose, and a gigantic cheek and neck.

I push my way out curving the bodies that surround me with the volume of mine and avoiding their immovable legs. A forest of Achille tendons, always hard and thin and standing in between place A, occupied by a body, and B, the exit of the bus. The butts are puffy and protruding like barricades that can't be lifted. Getting off the bus is like throwing yourself off a cliff. It's pretending that the stillness of the bus and the moment of your jump will match up. Everyday to endure the feeling of having 80 new uneven pairs of butts, Achille tendons, purses and people on the phone to rub against, overwhelms me, floods my senses.

II. EROS

A bulging crotch near my face exhaling the steam of its groin and a knit bag is hanging over my legs. Ever since she got on, I could smell the sweat and something else. Something that I could swear was weed. I can see she is tense, but... the stranger's crotch is close to my face. Mischievously inevitable thoughts of myself sucking it off enter my mind. This messy pile of people and chairs beating each other along the road in this metal box, gets eroticized. Somebody moves and dislodges the space the crotch's owner occupies, making his hard leg press against my shoulder.

III. INQUISITIO

You get on this paralelepípedo and pay for an hour so you can practice sleeping while standing, rub against your neighbor while your body argues the accident of movement, you learn to type on your phone with one hand, and with the other, you hold onto the pole like an ape and feel the solid ocean of glutes flowing behind you. You pay $0.38 and for two hours you can rent a torture device which massages your ankles with its hundred stilettos until you cannot feel them anymore. When time is up, the operator of the rolling torture machine offers to extend the ride and continues non-stop up to his home.

IV. COW

The red and green colors emitted from stoplights, and cars, spread until they crash against the windows scuffed by the rain and they obtain a vague asymmetrical texture. The windscreen wipers screech in a compulsive obsession to wipe off the texture but they cannot flatten the fog on the other side. Cows. Cows, we are cows ruminating on our sounds. Our silence. Our respiration. The rain makes us overcrowded like a pile of old toys forgotten in the attic.

We complain about this universe that we are creating and of how it avoids the laws of physics, but the truth is that we are looking for smothering contact with others. We hate each other to the point in which loneliness and hate make us want to die by ripping the air out of each other's lungs. Like chickens pecking at each other. Cows. Each day we go back and forth to the slaughterhouse, barely conscious. And there we go all dead, hanging from the poles, piled up on chairs that make us seem alive.

V. PNEUMA

Be careful when opening the upper compartments. Heavy objects could fall. But then they open them, and cows fall, and cows fall, and cows fall, a waterfall of cows, and they fall hitting us with their cold legs, and their fur, dead yet not withering.

VI. DOG

A dog, roadkill on the highway, exists. It is a possibility of being, of matter. For the matter also is. And it has states of being. Like that, with its guts in overlapping plates, out of their initial purpose, and its bones that do not have volume anymore and its lumpy fur.

VII. GRID

The ancient painters and sculptors since the Egyptians would enclose the human body within grids, made equivalences, calculations, traced lines, and cut their models in half, as the magicians do to their assistants. And like the magicians, they created an illusion. They can open corpses, study anatomy, do foreshortening, maybe even cure a few diseases on the way, but that won't make us any less uneven or disproportionate. Hunchbacks of Notre Dame. The owls have one ear noticeably higher than the other, a feature that makes them have a more panoramic hearing. It makes it easier for them to listen to their prey or predator. We humans are not owls, we do not make that frightening noise at night —sometimes, we snore— but our ears are as misaligned as the ones of the owls. Symmetry is different from efficiency. Our eyes are not aligned either. They are not the same size; they are not perfect spheres. We are far away from the angelic world. The world of the angels that we create in our image and resemblance. Or in our *dis-image* and *dis-resemblance.*

From our disparity. Our abdomens cannot be divided into two equal parts, our potpourri of intestines (Yes, I said potpourri), are diverse, and cannot be distributed in the same form. And every gut is unique. Not even a liver is equal to another. Just like not one brain is the same as another nor functions the same as any other. Just like no fingerprint looks like any other. The models. They make them seem like goddesses. However, it is all filters. Just the camera. Just lighting. An ensemble of lights. Each model has one eye bigger than the other, one lower than the other, one further away from the camera than the other, one leg fatter than the other and the disparity of their intestines deforms their stomach ever so slightly. In the end, they are just a pile of muscles, guts, veins, arteries, nerves, ganglia, and bones. A vanishing point will never abolish chance.

Un point de fuite "jamais n'abolira le Hasard." Jamais!

VIII. ILLUSION

Why do we even believe that we are human beings? Why do we believe that we are atomic beings (If "atom" means "indivisible")? We are fabulous ogres, chimeras. We are constructed in the image of monadic animals. That is why we are not like primates; we never have been. Our skeletons, perhaps. But our skeletons could also, by chance of science, have been named descendants of tigers or mammoths. We all have ribs and four limbs. Yet dressed in different skins, hair, make-up, clothes, glasses, and other various prosthetics, we are infinite hybrids. And we look like other animals. We look like flies, pigs, tigers, turtles, even like manatees. Some tend to look like one animal, others like another, but in the end we all are but children of Dr. Moreau. If we look patiently in the mirror, we can even see our seams: the bull sown to the pig, to the panther, to the baboon. We are not too far ahead of other species: agriculture, architecture, courtship, the family, the social castes, they were all invented by other species. Even languages. Wolves, ants, bees, dolphins, even meerkats, they are all way ahead of us. They have created their own perfect infallible systems. They can even transform. Make a house out of saliva—or a trap—, all by themselves. Make their wings grow. Or lose them. Let's be realistic, we call it instinct because we envy them. However, we did develop something unique. We have invented mythologies only so we can inhabit them. All living creatures are perfectly sealed monads. Us humans are a broken monad instead, and even if we are put back together we will never be the same.

All the king's horses and all the king's men couldn't put Humpty together again.

THE FOOT

*Translated by Karen Ortega
and Priscilla Ortiz*

Our house looks so much like a pigpen that my old dog Bruno gets confused and pees on the floor, treating the living room as an outdoor patio. That room inhabited by my mother's shadows and tears has now become a patio covered with the last few pieces of furniture we owned. My house, well, our house, now goes through a shivering tunnel, like a great vagina made of time and no time. Our home and everything that lives in it.

One might say: time, vicious and hungry, has been devouring the furniture and even my bones. Every day there is less furniture, less clothes, less things in the house. And slowly, as the days pass,...

I, myself, am becoming less and less.

Since the fracture, it felt like something had drifted away from me, and I don't know if it will come back. I don't know exactly what I lost, but every day I feel less like myself. Perhaps I will lose it forever; perhaps a new legion of it will come to dwell within me, as it happens with old houses. An architect comes with the arrogance of a Parthenon or pyramid builder and knocks everything down, peels the walls, rips the floors, and little by little undoes the old atmosphere of the house. He constructs a place so empty and cold that it does not retain echoes but reverberates them through the walls, without any memory or dreams, until other people come. Maybe then, the house won't remember its former owners.

So here I am, hoping for new times, new images, and new desires to dwell within me just like this house. Currently, I have no dreams. I resign myself to this endless falling and cracking; to this fracturing of myself.

And my future husband, whom I wonder if is even excited about our wedding, remains there, trying to look me in the eye, and I look back at him, empty. So empty that I don't even notice if he's empty too. Which is why I told him we should elope without all the noise. Noise is like a muscle that hurts when I try to move it for the first time. Pain is a reaction to the unknown. At least, that's what the physical therapist told me the other day when I tried to do an exercise and it hurt so much that my soul ached.

My soul.

But wait, I was talking about noise. Marriage is meaningless noise; love is true silence. Sometimes silence is so deep that it becomes inexpressible. Sometimes you fall in love and don't know it, and you feel and think so many things without noticing.

That's why I love being alone in my room, sometimes doing nothing but staring at the wall. There I just ramble senselessly, letting the images, sensations, and smells come to me. It's not that I am happy there. I hardly ever feel happy. But at least when I'm alone I try not to second guess myself if I love or don't love, want or don't want, or will or won't do. Sometimes I do wonder. But I do my best not to find an answer. Sometimes I say the wrong answers. Sometimes all I do is doubt.

Last night, for example—well, technically, it was dawn—an irrational fear assailed me, and I started questioning if getting married was the right thing to do. So I doubted and doubted many times and even doubted my own love. But again, whenever I ask myself those things, I get them wrong.

I was so carefree as a child, in my own world, exploring myself and others, trying to find answers to everything without asking anyone. These days, that place is so far away and so deep inside me that it is unreachable. Even though as a child, I could spend hours there without getting bored. I was so entertained by myself that I would ignore the people around me. I would even forget to speak. I even forgot that I was a person that had legs and arms; I forgot my own face, my own name, and my own gender. Then I would go to the mirror and look at myself for a while, disgusted with my appearance because that was not what I saw when I spent all that time immersed in that world. Within my true self, I had no body, no gender, no face, not even a name. Absorbed in the primal substance.

It still happens. And it is not an escape from reality. The escape is when I return to the world. There, where I am forced to be happy for everything, and every action is carefully performed so I don't offend anyone. Laugh, follow the conversations, act "appropriately", and own things, and manage my money, and love others. At times, I ask myself if I love because I "love", or if I love because it's the right thing to do. Matrimony is the "correct" thing to do, and it's what people expect of each other. When you don't have a man and don't get married, it is a tremendous disappointment for the whole world. They even stop calling you, and everyone believes that you go on to live in a sad, dark, and bitter sphere of unfinished lustful desires. It makes me uncomfortable to be around people more preoccupied with their posture and that of the others, and their use of silverware and the grooming of their phrases to impress others. Why not regard the sunlight that seeps through the window, or the planetary conjunctions, or good literature? Or what about sharing the dark moments they have lived through? I only think about what happened to me, the unutterable, what can only be written, but never be said. God has made spoken languages in such a way that, when you try turning the deepest spiritual truth into words, it will always sound ridiculous. That is why man had to invent writing. That is why what is sacred must be written. There is where it finds its precise and just solemnity. For example, if I say out loud that: "I'm falling apart like the walls of this house," everyone will tell me not to talk like that, or to think about those things. But if I write it down, they will say, "oh, what a beautiful simile!"

We should be more like Bruno. If a room smells like death, we could pee on the empty cabinet in the corner, and that's that. Perhaps this is how we exorcise the ghosts that haunt us. Perhaps that's what he did. In the face of this slow invasion of ghosts, peeing is a more immediate way of expressing our discontent, our fear. In this house, ghosts enter through the roof, and we excuse them by saying they are leaks. Because we find it hard to believe that the dead are taking shapes as precise and pure as drops of water. We find it hard to think that instead of talking to us, they drip and hit the bottom of the buckets that we put on the ground to contain them.

And lightning strikes, breaking through the roof. It leaves its dark stain on the carpet, and we insist on blaming the laws of physics so we are not possessed by fear in front of the cold and perverse waterfall that comes roaring down from the ceiling, ruining books and furniture that once belonged to our grandparents. We try to convince ourselves that we are fine, and those were just things that we lost. However, we always forget that our bodies are like the furniture and books and porcelain in the house; they are a tiny part of us.

My mother and I used to be the pillars of the house. Then, she died, and her soul departed so suddenly that I could not hold the roof up by myself. Not even the things. Creaking, cooling, little by little, every piece of furniture began to crack. Now we live under a constant avalanche of things breaking apart and getting wet. And I walk around the house, insisting that all this can be explained by the laws of physics, but sometimes my movement is just an illusion, as the body is nothing more than a part of oneself. Similarly, when one goes outside their depths into the real world already believing that they will become a "normal" person, trying to become one of the pieces that fit into society. But the soul is not a doll you can carry around inside a stroller, as much as the soul communicates with the world, it can't dwell anywhere else but deeply within. No matter how much I write, there will always be something ineffable left. Beyond any language. The soul was never born so it could express itself. The soul was never born. Period.

That is why, the certainty of love, or even the certainty of desire, doesn't come easy. I already stopped asking myself. I just do the right thing. What everyone expects of me, or what no one expects. But I act outwards. Because if I acted for myself, I would be at a standstill. I would stay in that place, which is not comfortable at all because it is the siphon of everything evil; the evil, that is, everything that makes you wonder. I would stay in that place, trying to feel what I truly am. That would seem more fruitful to me than acting like everyone else does, like mannequins in a showcase, trying to strike a pose that best suits the clothes they are forced to wear.

That is why this house stopped being a house and became a river. And that's why my foot stopped being a foot and became a stone that hurt.

TWENTY ARMS
Translated by Priscilla Ortiz

Once upon a time, in a long-lost kingdom, there was a princess looking for a prince. If her suitors had less than twenty arms, she would cut off a pair. But because she was so beautiful and virtuous, many would cut off their own arms just to get a glance of her beauty.

The projector stopped working.
It was the beginning of the machine's rebellion.
It wasn't a power move, it was abandonment.

Translated by Karen Ortega

MAX

Translated by Ian Finley

The trembling of his jaw as he scratches his swollen, worm-filled belly will be one of the things I remember best. This is especially true now, as everything around me seems to dissolve, stretching the boundaries of reality. When he and I met, it had to happen on the highway. He was on his way to the Kingdom of the Dead and I was on my way back from it. The first thing that we saw was his head, his small ears bent forward. Although it doesn't make sense, I swear that I could see the sweetness in his eyes miles before our paths crossed.

There were three of them, all extremely skinny, their bellies bulging like balloons, swollen and on the verge of bursting, the hips settled on arrowheads like tributes to La Santa Muerte.[1] They were so small, we tried to save them all. One bit my finger and ran away, a second followed, and both disappeared into the wilderness. I could not fathom where they got such energy. We turned one last time, and from the van we could see their bewildered heads, their wild eyes fixed on us. We tried to approach them once more, but they ran back into the bushes and didn't return.

Max jumped into my arms, then settled on my lap and closed his eyes. It was as if he saw me as solid ground, or, worse, he feared abandonment like a prisoner on his way to the gallows. When he arrived home on Saturday night, perhaps his first night among humans, he slept at the vet's. Every colony of microorganisms,

1 A reference to the Mexican cultural icon Our Lady of Holy Death, notable for her expanding cult following and skeletal appearance.

every piece of the ecosystem that sheltered his body, was dislodged. He had to give up being a solar system of his own to live in our world. We found him on December 22nd and he came home with us on the 24th. He was our modest Christmas gift, just as we were his. He was so meager that he barely existed among the living. We couldn't tell if we had rescued a fox, dog, or fawn. And what if one day we found him with a couple of *pudu*[2] antlers? Or perhaps feathers instead of hair? The poor thing had some patches of dried fur that looked like freshly-burned grass. Looking at him, one could not tell whether he had front legs or malnourished wings.

There was an entire ecosystem in more than just his insides. Under his skin, there were citadels scattered here and there, protected under pale domes, the inhabitants of which appeared to be bustling with endless tap dancing, as he always had a constant, exasperating itch. Max was so weak that the veterinarian refused to repeat the dose of the antibiotic on him. And yet, when you passed your fingers through his skin you would find those domes: some soft, others like stiff fortresses. You would find thickets of hair, hard like withered weeds and glued together by dry pus. When you passed your hand through this hard, dry valley of bones barely lined with skin, you would feel sick, then would reflect in the oases of his eyes and know that, nonetheless, everything would be alright.

His teeth indicated that he was, after all, a dog, and that he was approximately two months old. He was so helpless and fragile; he ate and slept, ate and slept. A few times he tried to bite my hand as if it were one of his mother's teats. Every time I left the room, he stood there, not making a peep. Knowing this, I never wanted to leave the room without him. I cooked with him in my arms, I ate with him on my lap: everywhere I went, he went with me. Soon the sickening sensation of touching his wounds grew into affection. I even ignored the symptoms of asthma that

2 The pudu (Spanish pudú) is the world's smallest deer, a species native to South America.

rekindled from the moment I held him in my arms in the middle of the road, even though they were supposed to disappear when the summer came. My porous mind hadn't needed motherhood: it gave in to the torturous pleasure of writing and that was enough. But now I had found a being that made me feel needed, one that licked my hand every time it came close as he knew he wouldn't survive without it. He never would have known what it was like to become a dog in this world. I realized that I was at once both empty and full of desire, both joyful and sorrowful. My mind was indeed porous, but there was something unknown, something ancient beyond my mind that overpowered my drive to create. What ruled me now was a drive to nourish.

So I watched his ears unfold, I watched how his scrawny limbs turned into strong paws as he learned to run, to want to run— transforming from the fragile world he was into a powerful sun. And so blinded was I by this sun that I could not see. I ignored the sores that were popping up on me each day; I ignored the pain that quietly overwhelmed Marco and me. Max was only seven months old when my first finger fell in the sink while brushing my teeth, and I had to rush to pick it up so that he wouldn't eat it. Days later, Marco and I were coughing up blood and keeping our severed fingers in the freezer. The doctors would have refused to mend those necrotic, pus-filled fingers—that's what Marco said. After all, he was a doctor himself. Because of this, we were confined as prisoners in our own house. It was hard for me to flash Max a toothless smile every time he ran between my legs wagging his tail. I didn't want to scare him. Now that breathing has become an arduous task, I wonder what will become of him when we're gone. Will he feed on our poor, diseased remains? I think of that fungus that attacks the carpenter ant of Brazil, making the insect climb to the top of a tree and clench onto the highest leaf or branch before it deploys a stem from the head of its host and releases a myriad of spores which float gracefully away to another host. Does the ant feel the same ecstasy that I do now when, with my last strength, I look at Max's eyes before I fade from the world completely?

No, it wasn't the skipping of a heartbeat,
what she felt this time
was an unbearable softness.

Translated by Ian Finley

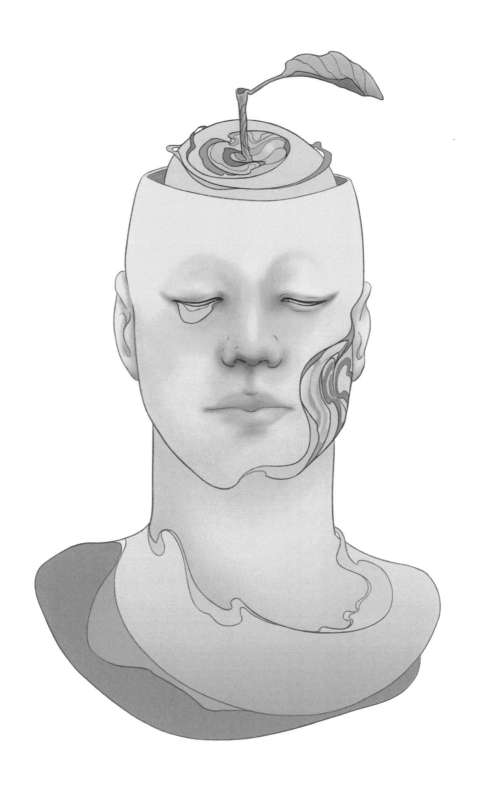

SEED

Translated by Kimberly D. Solis

She had left. He knew it because her silence was gone. All that remained was her absence. Her silence was red and yellow. She thought with fear and urgency. Her thoughts left an aroma of tears and anger. When she left it was like those short moments when the city stops thinking, when the lights go out and all that remains is a white silence. Such was the silence in which he could finally hear his heart. Those short moments made him feel free, free like a bird. When she left it was also his freedom, a melancholic freedom, a white freedom, stripped of her scent. She smelled like ginger and pain and to feel her was to enter her memories, because all living beings smell of what they remember and live. Sniffing was a way of knowing and every thought smelled different. The thoughts of other dogs were large balls, dense fluff defined by flat colors, but human thought always reached him in triangles, circles, cubes, made of soil, of seawater, of river, and of the strange, and ancient yet new machines. He liked being around humans so he could smell them. They produced beautiful harmonies of aromas so full of helplessness with small intervals of victory...

So when she returned, with the excuse to play between her legs, he put his nose up to her crotch, making sure to moisten it, tuning it before listening to the music. Because all living beings think better with their genitals. Trees, for example, in their slowness of life and breath, incubate their thoughts until petals come out. Sometimes they think sad thoughts that attract many insects and worms, and let themselves be eaten whole. That is their way of getting erased. But when they don't, their thoughts are happy. Soft and sophisticated happiness. Every flower is a slight shade of that thought. They then get excited. And then they get serious. They repress the emotion behind their cheeks and the idea becomes so dense, so YES, that they have to release it round and nourishing to the mouths of birds and other animals. They agree at first. They swallow it with gluttony. Then they conclude that they are crap, but the trees, although sad, keep releasing their ideas. Because they are the only beings on the planet that give life by giving ideas. Just like the first delicate thoughts disguised as petals, those whose nectar feed bees and flies, the last thoughts are whole and filling. Those last thoughts, one must add, they say: "Live. Like that but even more"; they say: "Tell me," and then they release those tiny eggs in which they are contained whole. Let's not deny it, he tells himself, a seed is the most perfect idea. That's why, when he receives the pit of the apples she leaves for him, he doesn't eat the seeds, because nothing deserves to thrive more than a perfect idea.

THE LAST NIGHT
Translated by Kimberly D. Solis

The heat melted the soles of her shoes to the asphalt. The black fumes of air were so hard to breathe. She felt heavy, a body without bones. Like a monster that disintegrated as it was touched by the heavy rays of sun. A slimy mass that rolled painfully down the sidewalk. There was not even a whisper of wind moving the branches of the trees. As much as she wanted, she couldn't make her legs move. It was as if she were trapped in a painting. The only thing that kept track of time was the air which dissolved the figures and turned them into a sea of phantasmagoria. Her shadow followed her dim and quiet, hopeless like her. For so long she tried to gather the pieces of her love. All these pleas, all these prayers to the soulless Sun and now it was falling towards the horizon, defeated. Oh, how small is your love, the dying star would have told her. Watch my vengeance. Although vengeance is not a good name for it, for celestial bodies are accidents and thus are all the subtleties of life.

The streets looked more empty than minutes before. The silence was stronger than the chirping of crickets. Silence and night, ultimate lovers, walked backwards through the deserted city hand-in-hand. Night walked ahead, untouched, ignoring the slow terror in the eyes of the dying souls. Silence followed a couple of steps behind, leading the parade of all his dark beings.

THE SHAPES OF AIR
Translated by Kimberly D. Solis

I put my trench coat on, not because I was cold, I just felt safe wearing it. Trench coats are like protective mothers. If it's raining, they protect us from it, carrying us to another world away from it; and if it's not raining, then you will be there the same, far from any danger. The sun came burning through the glass door and I moved my foot towards the beam of light just to feel as if my whole body was lying on that small bright square on the floor. A yellow-bellied fly landed on my knee, and for an instant it hit me: time is but a transparent substance that moves us. I witnessed the shapes of air, spiraling like courting birds under the sun.

ARIADNE

Translated by Dolores A. Melchor
and Kimberly Rodriguez

As she sat in the Metrolink, she did not care if her seat was hot or cold. She never believed that the great diseases of humanity could be transmitted by the heat left by a stranger's behind. She is an atheist. An atheist of science, atheist of television, atheist of politics. This trinity is the opium of the people. Better said, the people are the opium of the people. She states science is a religion because it's based on truths that one could believe or not, refutable as they are; equations often crushed by other equations; facts that will never be objective, because mankind cannot be objective. Only the object can be objective. Science makes you a fanatic, like any religion, like any soccer team. People in the Middle Ages forgot that the Earth was round. Science said that we lived on an *arepa*[1] from whose edges the sea dived, suicidally into infinite emptiness. They also forgot that nothing falls in the void, just floats... like ignorance.

Television, dot-dot-dot, she refers to television as a diabolical box. She calls it diabolic even though she does not believe in the Devil. The television founded its own religion. It reduces the perfect sphere of the eye into a cube, each time flatter and more rectangular. It tells its followers that, if they imitate the modern version of the Greek statues; spray-tanned, wearing bikinis, and full of Botox, they can become angels.

---

1 Colombian tortilla made of corn.

The imported *tetrapack*[2] are the Great Book. All the main characters are their prophets, capable of forgiving an offense in five minutes and accepting their own mistakes in another two or three. *Dallas, Dynasty,* and *Bonanza* tell the story of our Disposable People, she says. But the Great Narrative is *The Clockwork Orange*, and Alex is the Great Messiah transmuted, like electricity into laser beams, just as celluloid strips into CDs. Alex is He Who Opens His Eyes, the one who manages to see the parade of headless chickens in a philosopher's colloquium. But this version of Alex, after one sip of the elixir, decides to decline, because there is no redemption for chickens.

She believes in Open Source, but not in *Hercolubus*,[3] nor in the Illuminati. She does not travel by train, but by *yutub*.[4] She does not *need nobody, nobody around*.[5] She looks at her breasts in the mirror, while she thinks about the fierce mono-pectoral *Amazons*,[6] sighs, repeating like a prayer, not so convinced: Amazon-dot-com, Amazon-dot-com, Amazon-dot-com. She buttons up her blouse. She goes to the kitchen and warms a frozen lasagna in the microwave. While the earplug cable hits her thighs, she goes back to the computer dancing and singing to the Skype ringtone: "boo-bee-boob, bee-boo-beep."

She doesn't care much for artificial hiking, nor wave pools, but she loves surfing through the sea of bytes. Rushing through

2 This comes from the Colombian slang "enlatados gringos", "yankee canned TV" referring to TV shows imported to Colombia national network.

3 It's a conspiracy theory from the 90s and 2000, written about in "Hercolubus the Red Planet" by V.M. Rabolú, that stated that a planet, really a meteorite, would collide against the Earth.

4 This refers to the song "I Don't Go By Train" by Charly Garcia. Although the author changes "train" to, as YouTube sounds in Spanish, "yutub".

5 The lyrics of the aforementioned song.

6 This refers to the single-breasted Greek characters who would cut off one breast so they could fire their bow and arrows more easily.

the Data Highways. Exploring the mazes of windows and links unseen.

Ariadne loves *copipeist*.[7] Why say things if many people have posted them already? Why work if *gúgol*[8] has the answers? "And the Word said, let there be light, and the rest gave a like and retweeted it."

This is how she has gotten to like her binary travels more, to the meeting in the virtual rooms of *Seconlaif* [9] where no one knows anyone. Where you can name yourself whatever you want, say what you have always wanted to say, upload pictures of Angelina Jolie or Chris Evans and at the bank line, no one will know that it's you who likes bondage or fisting or *geronto-necro-zoophilia*[10] or suddenly *zoo-chocoramo-philia*.[11]

Her "real" life has become a mere shadow of herself. She foregoes the human voice, each day a bit more. When the phone rings, she is sure that it's the bank, or that they're offering her a promotion, and so she never answers. All day, her house multiplies the echoes of the sound of her fingers typing on the keyboard. And she multiplies herself in chat windows, blogs, and Google searches. Multitasking. That way she can love simultaneously, know simultaneously, post simultaneously against bullfights, comment on her 2543 *feisbuc*[12] friends' status, watch videos in Hindi, and finish writing that story that she started three years ago.

7 Copy-paste.

8 Google.

9 Second Life.

10 A play on words with gerontophilia, necrophilia, and zoophilia.

11 Chocoramo: a brand of chocolate-covered cake typically from Colombia.

12 Facebook.

When Ariadne has to go out to the overcrowded street, with the dusty wind blowing into her eyes and the disapproving looks of people, she hates doing it alone. She prefers calling a friend and asking them to join her. That way it hurts less. She prefers her loneliness when accompanied by the written words of strangers when no one is looking her in the eye.

Her real voice and face are only for her old friends. Speaking in front of the prying eye of the webcam is like having a conversation with someone in a mirrored cafeteria and watching each other while talking, while sipping coffee, while distrusting, while loving, while imagining. Her face changes imperceptibly with every dream or with every bit of hate that creeps onto her lips. And it vacillates between thousands of emotions and expressions every minute; and if only we were aware of every second, we could witness those little miracles.

"Real" sex is for her lovers. She saves all the *clousaps*[13] and all her vulnerability for them. She saves her naked, animal desire for the silent and cruel eye of the camera. For it, for them, she allows herself to remember her past as a female, where she frantically procreates at the edge of the hostile precipice of extinction. She savors the *sensoteca* (sensory archives) that has been constructed in her head. She chooses to imagine a kiss. That current that runs from between her legs to the navel and from the heart to the head. She then imagines the scent of the other, the smell of their breath, their sweat, their body. She doesn't care if what she imagines will become true or not. She just likes to feel what her mind creates for her. It is the perfect combination of the highest sensations caused by all her past lovers.

She remains alone, surrounded by air and a bit further away, the screen. Bytes. The other teleported in pixels folded against the wrinkles of her face in ecstasy. Only then does she yearn for the skin. Only then does she realize that she has forgotten

13 Close-ups.

the smell of saliva. That she has not kissed anyone physically in years. That she has only given digital kisses. Then she goes back to her memories and there she stays because she no longer knows how to speak in front of three-dimensional people of flesh and blood. What makes the difference is language. Words, according to their weight, their ductility, their magnetism, their electrical charge. She has fabricated a *sensaciómetro*[14] in the tiny valve in place that prevents her from locating her electrons while measuring their velocity. And like with electrons, such elaborate mental apparatus tries to measure, weigh, calculate, subdivide the intricate anatomy of words. Words which her eyes weave as they appear, released pigeons, in the chat window. If they say, "hello beautiful," she shudders. She imagines the tone and timbre of the voice. She equalizes it on the left side of her brain. She touches it on the left side. Due to the decussation of the pyramids. So many years ago, when she was a schoolgirl, the biology teacher wouldn't explain what this phenomenon was. That is why, because it is mysterious and mystical, she likes to use it in her poems.

Sarcasm turns her on. Sarcasm rhymes with orgasm. She likes the anticipation. And it makes her brain feel like a tree blooming with electricity. But she does not fall in love with those who say it. The sarcasm enters from below. From the cord of her coccyx. And stays spinning in the base of her spine. Sarcasm is an infrared word that only reaches red and orange. If anything, yellow. But poetry... poetry is something else. It takes no time to get into her head. It is lightweight and it is lead, it remains in the threshold between worlds. That's why Ariadne must chase her, catch her as she flies, say the magic word that opens the upper hatch of

the vessel of her body, and get it into her head, dripping colors until they all turn into violet and purple. There, the poem strikes through her from head to toe and then stays, like a spark, like an indigo bullet, bouncing within the chambers of her heart, competing against the drum of her pulsar. That is why she has

14 Like a thermometer but a sensory-meter.

not touched her lovers for a long time. Because she knows that those who weave clouds are like ghosts, like unborn children: they are deep within themselves. They live raw like an open wound. Her mision is to steal the Fire every day. They cannot be touched. They walk with a quill, stabbing others in their rib cages. It is their job. They understand pain. But they can't stop themselves from causing it. They suffer and they want the whole world to suffer with them. She knows it. She is also a weaver.

THE DRAGONFLY AND TIME
Translated by Alejandro Murillo

A dragonfly is fixated on following a path, but the windy breeze surpasses her will. Let the wind take you. Air is time. Air cures and heals. Air has no sense of where to go. You are air. Time is unpredictable. Time is but a multiplicity of streams clashing and dancing with each other. You are air.

LEIBNIZ AND ARCHIMEDES
Translated by Rebeca De La Cruz

What if the bus that I'm riding slams into that truck in the lane beside us, with two wagons full of cows? Upon the collision, the linear path that we're following will fall into disarray; and all the material and organic bodies, upon micro-colliding against each other, would create their own course, would be linear, folded, orbiting for an instant around the point of greatest force of collision, and would form, with that line, a figure that would be an instant representation of fear. An ephemeral artwork of nature. With every piece orbiting that point, continuous or contiguous to each other, a figure is formed, almost geometric. They would belong to a greater center of gravity (the point of collision between both vehicles), and other more localized centers of gravity (the bodies colliding with each other) —for a moment or two, a microsystem; and then they would belong to nothing anymore, not even themselves—chairs, cans, bones, feet, cell phones, wallets—no longer objects and living beings, yet still belonging to the material world. The souls, in the ever-dynamic process of destruction and dissection and multiplication and division, would always be preserved in a fragment of their original form; or maybe they will experience entanglement, multiplicity equivalent to the separate parts. In that way I could be unity (if my head, or better yet, my torso survives) and many (in case they don't).

SLAUGHTER
Translated by Alejandro Murillo

I can't recall where I was, that moment when I witnessed the slaughtered pig and his huge dead figure lying on the trailer's bed. The lifeless mass jolted on the truck's bed as it bounced over potholes down the street. I was four years old; the pig and I were four years old, and we were dead. The pig, deceased, yet still affected by the laws of physics, as his soulless body traveled down the road, the vivid image of its bright red blood running down the truck's bed ran through my mind. Maybe I was the one being tied up on the rails alongside the pig in the back of the truck. We were young and ultimately, it was difficult for us to grasp the full picture of what we had witnessed. We had a close-up view, we focused solely on life while everything else faded away in the background. The image of my death was so recurring that it multiplied in my memory. Sometimes it's through my bedroom window of that old house in Teusaquillo. Sometimes I'm looking through the rear window of my grandfather's car. Sometimes I'm standing in a random corner of the city, watching it. The setting from where I'm being observed changes every time. At times even the shades of the surrounding light, the temperature of the air aren't consistent, yet I still live through that enormous pig made merely of meaningless fragile tissue tied to thin lines of silence. It's safe to say that some of our cells did not know of their decay yet they kept performing their mitotic dance, working arduously to produce liquids, proteins and serotonin for who knows how long. My aunt believed I had been traumatized by this experience when instead I was only trying to understand what the red liquid that flowed off the truck was, trying to grasp the quietness and peacefulness of the deceased pig. I recall seeing all that, even though it happened within a second of the livestock truck passing by. I had no idea what was in my sight as I only remember seeing the giant piece of discolored skin decorated with black and red trickles of blood. The surrounding adults murmured, "poor little girl, she has just seen a dead pig, poor girl will be scarred for life." First thought that came to my mind was, "this is big, so I should remember this forever." I didn't foresee the suffering preceding death. Instead I processed the eternal ecstasy that flowed from the lifeless body, which remained the same as when he lived, but carrying behind his name, his pain and any of his futures, with such a potent backwash, yet still invisible to everyone. Witnessing the start of its composition, its incommunicability to the outside world, with disregard to the plaintive and disturbed opinions of adults, had been a gift for us.

DO NOT STOP
Translated by Dolores A. Melchor

You are driving along an intermunicipal road in the middle of
The night and you see a sign ahead that says:

CAUTION
WOMAN IN
WEDDING DRESS
100 M
DO NOT
STOP

NORMA

Translated by Rebeca De La Cruz

Every day, Norma Jean wakes up with her mother's words echoing within the walls of her head, swinging from the membranes of her arachnoid mater: stupid girl. Stupid girl.... On the way to the location, she keeps telling herself that her mother was wrong. She remembers seeing her own glowing face gracing the billboard of her latest movie, and spitefully thinking how much she would love for her mother to see it and then choke on her own bitter words, one by one. Stepping out of the car, as the dust settles at her shoes, she waves hello to a couple of girls that work as extras for the new movie and she quickly realizes how much they think they know about her, how much they admire her and expect of her. She smiles, trying to hide her trembling lips, pull herself together, and keep in mind their admiration. As she walks toward her trailer, she bumps into her co-protagonist. Her co-protagonist, *copro-tagonist*, she repeats to herself, realizing that no one else would understand that joke—her "Prince Charming," to whom they probably had to give several cups of coffee at the last minute to get him ready for today's scenes—maybe something stronger. Ugh. Today we shoot the kiss, she thought to herself while casting a quick glance at his full, disgusting lips. If she could separate the man from the character who's going to kiss her, she just might feel like she's in love. That's her job. Get into character. Distance herself. Split. Be someone else. Fall in love. But in that moment, she could see naught but the gay alcoholic who forces himself to sleep with women to establish a façade. In that moment, she can only loathe him for his mediocre, slimy kisses, and his bad breath. At the end of the day, they are no different; they both lead double lives. She forces herself to feel helplessly in love again and again, floating on the clouds again and again, seeing purity in the eyes of a man again and again, ignoring the contempt, keeping the questions that no one's going to answer and the jokes she invents to herself.

She's learned this the hard way. Today she is a blonde girl, and blonde girls don't ask questions. They pout, they roll their eyes, and they shake their hips.

Her body is hard to ignore. That's what the pictures in the newspapers and the captivated glances of men say. However, in front of the mirror, she doesn't see anything special. In front of the mirror, she just sees a defenseless, ordinary woman. Maybe the director has finally figured her out. This is like the tenth time that he has repeated it in front of everybody: You are getting worse every time. How can you possibly be so bad at acting! But she's learned to save her tears, to postpone them, until recess. She then runs to her trailer, into the magnanimous jaws of her purse, to rummage through its intestines, so full of blessings. There, where those tiny tickets to silence and eternity await her. Because each look and each word is nothing but a multiplied reflection of her mother's heart, once slammed against the floor and broken into pieces, then poorly glued back together, and then thrown at her to break her own heart. Only one of those pills, washed down with a sip of champagne, is able to patch her up, and remind her of what she was like before she broke down. With every sip, her mother, and all those who had ever contemplated her, trickle down her esophagus and burn in the acid of her forgetfulness. They are scalded in bubbles, they get cauterized. She could fold her fears, neatly, one by one, and bury them deep at the back of her mind. She could open her eyes and gaze into the eyes of her Nemesis at the other side of the mirror—the beautiful, unattainable, empty Marilyn Monroe.

CLOUDS
Translated by Alejandro Murillo

She lies belly faced to the sun, lingering under the plants that shrivel with the roaring heat of the midday. Fixing her sight onto the clouds that lurk around the roof tiles of the houses down below. The Earth underneath passes by, giving its last glance to the imperfect fractal borders of the clouds.

In Bogota, there's always a gray cloud over her head. She can't help but imagine that there's a possibility that even those grey clouds flow as their way of relaxation. They seem to be far less dense than other times she's seen. They are light, like cotton candy. The clouds begin to fade as the burning hands of the tropical sun press against her face and her bare chest, slowly leaving a tan mark on her skin.

She remembers the heat of being an atom, and the electricity from being a single cell.

She asks herself how the anatomy of a cloud can survive in constant disintegration. She questions whether there's an existing awareness of being a cloud, or even a single tiny water drop condensed among many other millions of droplets, like a planet in the galaxy that floats randomly in space, hanging from the hair of the wind.

She wants to hold her pen. If she does so, if she writes down what she sees, if she glances for a single second at the piece of paper, then a crucial moment from the clouds journey through the sky might slip away. Then she won't be able to feel the aura of the sun on her skin. Then she'd be turning her back at the powerful yet mystified design looking at her from above. Twirling a billion times, fading away and gathering once again, the symmetry it seeks will never be fully comprehended by her. She will never see but a tiny part of it. Clouds will always appear to her as undefined shapes shifting upon her eyes.

THE STUDY OF CÉZANNE'S STUDY OF MONT SAINT-VICTOIRE
Translated by Monica Alonso

The volcano overlooks the village impassively. People live there and breathe the air from the volcanic god, ignoring that one day they will be buried under layers of his lava. One day, the volcano was a sphynx and devoured entire cities. The next day, he became a soulless monster with nothing but patience.

Today, he sleeps with his head tucked in the clouds. Perhaps he's hiding antique libraries. He's no longer interested. Only the trees know of his intentions, but the rest of nature doesn't, not even the birds.

He is a cold breast of Mother Nature so close to her burning heart. Everything—trees, houses, people—becomes a blur when he dreams. He even forgets about the tickling sensation all over his body and the extension of his being across the Earth, the floating speck of dust.

In the past, when only birds and pumas dwelled there, life was diaphanous. She understood the illusion of time. She felt the infinite number of other volcanoes, although they were peaceful at the time, peaceful after the Great Wrath and the Great White Depression. Long and green, each second grew and slipped through the grass in the empty space. They multiplied in the ice that housed the fish living at the foot of the volcano.

It was beautiful to dream and be one with the No. The No that was white, silent, and fluid. The No that wasn't a word but an endless snore. All the words of the soft songs of birds, and the cracking of their wings, their notes between the teeth of the tigers, were overtaken by the arrival of humankind. It was a happy death, but that day within the day, the center of the great speck of dust yearned for language.

The drunkenness of Nature makes time stand still.

SCHRÖDINGER'S BATHERS
Translated by Monica Alonso

I am the artist that paints me. I am the ideas that I can put into words. I am the colors. I am those endless sounds of waterfalls that were obscure to him, the waterfalls that caused him such an indescribable terror, the same ones that encouraged him to pick up my long and thin body, the paintbrush that I am. With the same color that gave *The Virgin of the Rocks* and *The Abduction of Helen* a subtle blush and the color used to paint Goya's nightmares and the red dragons painted by the copyist monk, I paint myself and I look at myself. "No man ever steps in the same river twice;" they bathe endlessly and once in the waters of time. All at the same time, everyone and no one bathes with Schrödinger's cat.

THE FOREIGN WOMAN
Translated by Monica Alonso

A man traveled to another world and from there he brought her. He traveled through the dark zone, the soundless zone, the zone without smell, without matter, he went and experienced the fear caused by the perfection of nothingness, and from there he brought her. He explored the zone and discovered what it was not to have a heartbeat, not to breathe, not to be, and from there he brought her. He brought her to live with him. A beautiful, silent woman. He invited his friends over to meet her, the woman with a big, generous shadow, a warm shadow that covered and cradled them like a mother, like a mother who does not love but is always there at the foot of the bed watching... watching... and everyone, without realizing she was incapable of love, feeling the slow embrace from her gaze that unsettled them, stayed bound to her by an enigma.

Every time they left, as soon as the door closed behind them, they felt like a weight had been lifted off their shoulders. They were happy as if they were children again, and the current day had been a blur of dreams that had not yet occurred. The friends who visited the man and the strange woman wanted to relive the peaceful memories of a happier past. The man who lived and slept with her every night also felt that peace at first. But then, mostly then, when the then was at night, when the moon was such a then and the stars appeared there to nostalgically embellish the sky, the man would close his eyes, and the woman, incapable of dreaming because her head didn't contain a rechargeable cyclic brain—because her brain held the entire universe within—, would watch him sleep. She loved him. He had liberated her from the non-dimension, the non-time. She loved the new world the man brought her to. Even so, she could not help but steal his memories. There was so much noise within him. So much sorrow piling up and she couldn't grasp how. In her world, there was no such thing as pain and there was nothing piling up. And there was nothing. She watched his dreams and found them repulsive with too much color. She was struggling to comprehend his real world which was her second world. The memories of what he lived through became entangled and formed frightening images that founded an entirely new third world for her. So, little by little, she meekly erased his dreams. He looked happier and happier each time he awoke. As the days went by, he started becoming more childlike because he could only recall the happy moments in his life and they were few. He remembered less and less every day; until one day, she had him exactly as she wanted. No longer sad, no longer happy, nothing, just like her.

A FIRE'S FABLE
Translated by Jocelyn Contreras

It was such a nonsense quarrel. I still cannot wrap my mind around how my brother ended up dying. I ask myself this question every time my eyes casually glance over at the tombstone facing our home. I wonder if it was worth unwinding, unraveling my rage. I won't deny, my brother Abel was a slacker and a complainer. His prayers would be devoted to an incomprehensible god whose solitary origins elude me. A god jealous of our gods. But... why murder him?

Sometimes I think that perhaps he and I were not really family. He would be found taming the seeds, while I was obsessed with stalking and hunting. He worshiped the Sun, while I preferred the cold, white light of the Moon that bathed me. It was as if my mother was ancient, wild, and unwilling to be controlled neither by mankind nor by the gods. As if reaching for the curved bone that once was the jaw of a beast, would lead me back to the hollow womb of the cave that once cradled me. Being the owner of the jawbone, the donkey had required all of my wisdom so I could understand him. Anyone who comes across a donkey is aware that, though they are portrayed as absurd creatures, it takes a wise man to break the silence of his submissive glare. Perhaps that is why, even after passing away, the creature had given me the sense of freedom, the same spark that he once had in his eyes.

Perhaps it took place on a musty hot evening in the ancient city of Nineveh; or perhaps it occurred in one of the walled cities of the Aegean Sea. It could have happened within each and every era, where we were both replicated continuously like in a house of mirrors. But what am I saying? I didn't know about mirrors. Or maybe...

All I remember is that the furious rage grew within me, boiling up my inner instincts. Was it a broken bowl? Was it because I refused to care for his crops? How foolish. The plants flourished back freely, and the gods provided us with everything. The memory of my brother's servile grimace, the hunched body, his eyes blinded by the sun, and the resonant sounds of the equine jaw against his skull. Did I know the round name of that rock of the head?

And the blood. The splatting of the blood, every warm drop splashing against my face.

My gods called it a sacrifice because being witnesses of it gave them pleasure. They wanted to award me a year of great hunting because I had lost the one and only thing that I had and loved. The god of my brother challenged my gods into a duel by fire. The winner would be the one with the most lethal fire. The fire of my god, the god of multiplicity, was powerful enough to bloom plants from ember. The fire of his god lit up the Earth and sky, and for a million years, everything would stop growing back. It was He that decided upon my destiny. His fire burned down all my temples and effigies, burned out the gold and scorched out all my forests. He left me like an orphan with nothing but charcoal and cinders. He sentenced me to wander the Earth without the chance of dying but also without life in a world dwelled by the roaring wheezes from His body in endless agony, for when He burned down the world, He himself scorched down to ashes.

APHID
Translated by Jocelyn Contreras

An aphid perceives the world as multiple, polymorphic. My body is perceived as a planet to him. Perhaps, that is how the earliest humans perceived the world around them, like an enormous god, with mountains as arms, with wrinkles on its surface: the humid rivers. Could this aphid perceive my inner self? How about my spirit? My wholeness? No. It would take him too much time. Perhaps, that is the way that our god works: a promise that is never kept. A journey back home, so yearned for that would turn into a promise fulfilled. Is that it? A return, perfected in a circle? Or is it a linear idea with such a need for a circle that it materializes it even if it's not meant to be? An aphid falls from its place on a tree, falls onto a hand where he partially observes the human face looking at him, with those eyes and nose. The aphid feels a sense of wind as would a Sherpa feel the Himalayan breeze. The Sherpa might believe that the frozen wind is blowing from an unknown god, unmoved by his pain. The aphid might believe that the wind messing with our hair is the breath of that god. The god, centered at the spherical nucleus, remains an unknowable mystery.

SUNROOTS
Translated by Jocelyn Contreras

I've killed a man. I cannot explain why. It has been my blood that fiercely poured out. My own mother cannot believe it. She claims that I am a good man. But she too knows, deep down, what we're made of. I've killed a man. I have heard his shrieks in my ear, his herbivorous breath pounding desperately against my knife. My body felt alive upon the drumming of his bones. I had never before killed a man, even though I had been in the dancing parade of my village many times. I'd never been a warrior nor a god. I'd never been a volcano nor a reptile. I've killed a man. Neither the cellmates in orange nor the guards in blue could comprehend. They hollered at me and called me sick-minded. They feared us, mother. They feared us, cousin. They expected me to kill a man. Now, they are grabbing me by my braid, my umbilical cord, they grab the sun tied to my back. They stab away the roots of the sun, crushing them to the ground. Killer Indian, killer Indian they holler at me while stomping on my braid, leaving me fatherless, an orphan to my feline god. I've killed a man.

PLANCK TIME
Translated by T. Logan Harrison

1. VOID

There was a time when I was a girl and barely even knew names for things, when I saw something profound—something solid, invisible, hanging in the air around me. I began to train my eyes in every way I could as I grew so I could see it.

I also suspected that, if I tried to look at things and faces through the corner of my eye, and I saw them foggy, half-formed, it was because reality was actually a plurality, and always imperceptibly changing. Some... years, decades, after, I learned about Planck Time and Planck's Constant: in terms of atoms, electrons take X time to complete one orbit around the nucleus. Enter the theory of Planck Time. The brain, seeing nothing where something should be, refuses to admit tardy particles, and moulds the illusion of reality. If the brain accepts this concept, we become shapeless, incomplete monsters in the mirror, speckled by black holes. We become voids between distant galaxies. Faces appear to us transparent and calm and yet they are crushed by the weight of corruption, as if burnt by acid. Cycling between who they believe they will be, what they want to be, and what they will never be. This tug-of-war is, as with the age-old rabbit-duck drawing, keeping us in an endless loop: is this a rabbit-duck-rabbit- duck-rabb...?

We are galaxies of inflexible consciousness. We are voids perpetually silent, for language is unknown to us. We are voids of dark matter, absorbing all sound in a blanket of lightweight, but dense carbon that engulfs us all.

5. (WISDOM OF) MEMORY

Sometimes, I say things that are completely against my own thinking, as though my mother is talking through me. Who then, actually, is my mother? I'm absolutely sure that anything I say these days is really her talking. There was even a period where I became fully convinced that she and I would be able to communicate with each other.

There was a foggy veil around my brain that, once parted, led me toward those who made me, and they who made them—all ensuring I can freely talk together with them.

3. UBIQUITY

The mirror may not be an illusion of light as much as it is an open window into another reality on the other side of the universe every time I look at it. I don't know what happens to the multiplicity of shadows behind the mirror when I step away. But I'm certain that when I look into my eyes, in its reflection my ubiquitous particles are multiplied into the other universe.

4. IN(DI)VISIBLE (ENDLESS CREEPING DOOM)

Every past, all futures, and each present mutilated by certainty, a monster that invades every closet plus the night itself.

1. ENTANGLEMENT (CERTIDUMBRE HECHIZADA)

The certainty that I could be boiled alive tonight, the sacrificial bull starting the French Revolution, or the Passover lamb's blood on the infidels' lintels. Pain is the only universal constant, the only lasting impression of our existence. The unquestionable doubt that, if I'm something other right now, it is because someone is watching me.

1 AND 0. WOULD YOU HAVE INSTEAD, A BINARY 6?

A 1 is allowed to be a shadow, a quill feather, or some retained sunlight on pavement. A 0, though, can halt time itself. That's how they act when they are being observed. They choose to be 1 and 0. They forget they were once every other number. They forget they were, each day, every day, every number.

2. PHOTOSYNTHESIS

My cells enjoy taking a break from humanity; it gives them time to perform essential photosynthesis.

6. CURVED SPACE-TIME

It goes without saying that, when you and I kiss, our ages unravel and all the kisses that have ever been shared are preserved in the ephemeral air between us.

0. ONE (INEVITABILITY)

All is in flux. Everything, at once, chooses to be 0, chooses to be 1. Close your eyes so you can feel me. I may steep myself in you, I am your twin. I am you. We are everything. We are 1. We are 0. We are the time it takes for an electron to orbit inside an atom of your skin. Inherently, an endless time where I, you, we, do not exist.

Planck time.

THE TRIUMPH OF WATER
Translated by Isabell Chavez-Munguia

My brother had to die in the water.

The day he died, we were all going out. It had rained for days on end and we were tired of being stuck inside the house watching it pour.

My mom, my sister, and I had all agreed to go out, which took a lot. My brother had also agreed. However, early that morning, around 6, he decided not to go. He had been invited next door for a cookout, and he would rather go there instead. I never saw how he was dressed, and I didn't hug him. The only memory I have left of him is him yelling, I'm not going! I'm not going! After my mom told him, you better be here at 5. I heard him slam the door. And we left.

It's incredible how one later tries to find any sign, a smell, the chirp of a bird, some number, something that would have advised us not to leave him alone that morning.

My brother had been lost for 14 days. The police and firefighters started the search; someone said they saw him play with the dogs on the edge of the river and lose his balance. The rain had left the ground slippery, and it was easy to fall. But he knows how to swim, my mother repeated; he couldn't have drowned. One of the divers who had gone down to search for him explained the river had gotten bigger throughout winter. My brother had worked in fish farming for 32 years; the constant trips to coastal places and lakes resulted in him acquiring fish-like skills. My brother decided to stop his studies when he was 14, and since then, until the day he died, he worked with fish, with their unique way of breathing as if they could talk.

One day they called us, about ten days later, to tell us that the divers had found a body. It had orange overalls and yellow worker boots. When they got him out, his head rolled, a useless organ, and it was never seen again. The bones were fragile, limp like overcooked spaghetti. They pulled out his body wrapped in a tight-knit fish farming net, to get the body out without it falling apart. They had just announced the news on the radio, and cars began to crowd the edge of the river. Entire families came to see if it was their late loved one. As the rescue team started to pull out the ropes with the body from the stream, the people started to wonder if what they would find at the end of those threads would lead to the end of their pain. It's a man, they said, and half of the people went back to their cars and back to nibbling away their hope and probabilities. When they had him lying on the ground, with his clothing faded but still in one piece, his fingers, dissolving into a stream of mud, they saw an ID in his pocket. The rest of the families got closer. That's my husband! shouted a lady. He'd been lost for ten years. It wasn't my brother. We went back home. The uneasiness that had left us that day started falling on us at the same pace of the night and the winter fog.

On the 14th day, they called us again, and we no longer wanted to believe. We preferred thinking perhaps he got tired of us, that he had left, or that he had died a different way, that his head, his fingers, his eyes were still intact, like that orange suit.

He was far from the place where they saw him fall, the river had dragged him a few kilometers. His body wasn't like that other worker's body. His lips and neck were blue, but besides that, his body wasn't swollen like they say happens when you drown. Besides how cold his hands and face were, it was my brother, and it looked like he could wake up at any moment.

My brother wasn't always like that, difficult, obsessive, stubborn. He wasn't always moody, nor did he have a short temper. He was hard-working, quiet, kind, he loved us and we loved him. When his boss called to tell us that he would bring him to Osorno,[1] because he was worried that my brother wouldn't eat and wasn't performing well at work, we couldn't imagine we would find him like that, so skinny, with such an invisible dark aura like an obscure cocoon all around him. Thirty-two days barely eating anything, his entrails turned into a void. We made him go to a psychiatrist, schizophrenia, he said. My brother developed the habit of taking about 23 showers a day. It was as if the water washed away time. As if the thing inside him, voices or maybe images I never asked, making him like a caged animal, would leave him thanks to the power of water. As if water were a weapon. He also smoked.

Two or three packs a day. Smoke and water, smoke and water, a persistent ritual of penance, of punishment, like an endless silent rosary. What tales he told to the whirls of smoke while they wisped away, I don't know; he stared at them squinting, I could swear, for just a moment, he felt some kind of happiness. Perhaps not; maybe he just wanted to die. Him, the athlete, the chatty one of the house, the one who would confront my dad when he was still alive. When we were kids, my dad would show up in the middle of the night drunk to beat us. My brother would lose every day a handful of words from the dictionary of his soul. It was sad watching him try hard to ask for cigarettes at the store down the block. Doña Berta already knew him. She would look at him, take a breath, smile, and would give him the box of cigarettes, she would take the money from his shaky pale hand and then she watched him walk away. Sometimes she would glance for a second at the water drops rolling down his face. My brother would not dry off after his shower. He would put on his clothes right then and there.

---

1 Osorno is a small town in Chile.

He was 41 the afternoon he fell into the river. He had his last meal, and I suppose his last showers, he went out with Apolo, Peco, Ernesta, Petunia, the whole pack of our adopted mutts. Whoever saw him play at the edge of the river and fall, I ask myself if they had also witnessed the sequence and all the subtle changes in the face that happens when one falls. The moment one loses their balance, feeling their legs give out from under them, and the next, when the whole body succumbs to the force of gravity. The mind yields to the fate of the body. Then, when the body acknowledges the chaos and the force of the water, the touch of the unknown brushing against them, one realizes there is no more air to breathe. And that the frantic Mother has embraced us in her womb.

THE BEGINNING: THE CHICKEN OR THE EGG?
Translated by Ezequiel Mata Jr.

While I see you die, it is God watching me. Maybe God is within the essential moment of someone dying. You can perceive it. Would it be cruel to take notes while in the presence of someone dying? Would you consider it an act of cruelty, or could it be a way to express grief? Everyone who I've seen die, animals and humans alike unfold the same aroma. Salty and bitter like deep-sea gardens. Just as if death had emerged at the same time as us mammals millions of years ago. That's the way it should be, after all death has been around since the beginning of Earth. Death is older. Besides, it must be as old as the Big Bang. Someone can assume that as soon as the Big Bang occurred it developed the need for the ocean, which led to a need for death. Death can have a penetrating smell because it is the scorching mark of the Beginning.

When death calls for us, the Big Bang pulls us back in. What was the smell of the moment just before that enormous explosion? Did it smell like nothingness, did it smell like hope, the same hope you can smell on a pregnant woman? The eyes are the windows to the soul. And everyone's souls are in the Big Bang, but we all lose that consciousness of being the beginning once we are alive. Living is so much work and it is so abundant that we take it for granted. Although we should be able to see the Big Bang in the eyes of someone who is dying. Because death slowly pauses time just like a flower closes at night. What can we find in the eyes of someone who is dying? Nothing. Nothing but darkness. Undoubtedly darkness. My dog might be dead tomorrow, or he might be saved. Every possible outcome would be an accident. The only thing that is not, is the Big Bang. The Alpha and the Omega. The Big Bang and the Big Crunch. Each second that I spend writing this down I refrain myself from contemplating the slow miracle of Death.

A DIALOGUE WITH "PLANCK TIME"

by Logan Harrison

1. VOIDED

Many, many years past when I was but a mere infant in comparison to my experiences now, I beheld something most profound—instinctively I knew it to be both significant and levying a good amount of importance the moment I was aware of it, although I was—at the time—unable to give it name or function within myself. In fact, the only physical form itself possessed was an indescribable impermeability in the air. Impermeable for absolute certainty then to my mind, but unable to be affected or swayed through touch, and not even a whisper of acknowledgement via sight, either; simply...there.

After some time during which I became accustomed to the force, I took it upon myself to train my senses any way I was able, to give my eyes the power to detect the entity which accompanied myself. By the point I reached this, there was usually a prescient sensation in the corner of my eye, waiting to be acknowledged at first, then foisting foggy, half-formed faces and ideas and semi-baked theories of others behind my eyes, and should I be incautious, given free roaming access to my consciousness when least I expected. Sometimes at points, I unwittingly phased through many dimensions and realities, which shifted almost before I knew it like tremors without my input or control, save, naturally, their aftershocks.

Following this shifting, entreating me from time to time as though unexpected houseguests left out far too much washing after they left—and sometimes they resided for decades before vacating my awareness—I was made aware of the theoretical concept of Planck time. Planck time, you see, describes the quantum and particle physics-based phenomenon and subsequent theory where, after a period of time X, such that a cluster of photons/electrons on their customary journey to the sun, are each prematurely delayed and prevented from completing their duty to the star for the duration. The brain, confronted with this affront to the universe, denies any access to perception of the atoms with enforced tardiness applied. However, if at some point the brain goes out on a lark and decides to see what happens when it (hopefully briefly) succumbs to the promised chaos well then. In this potentiality, we would then see a glut of half-formed near-incomprehensible monsters, devoid of any constrained shape, as though reflected by antique mirrors speckled throughout by narrow seedling voids on top of all else, constantly shifting with aspirational agitation. Were we to tunnel through these infant-multidimensional wormholes of promise, our adventuring senses would in hopeful theory see vast spaces filled with stunning galaxies many realities distant from our own, still very much detectably discrete, and at least partially unfinished, unformed, brimming with potential.

Faces we would (otherwise) see with openly trusting, perfect clarity are instead brought to our senses festooned with shadow, corruption, and incomprehensibility so severe it is akin to acidic burns. These afflictions visited upon the clarity, you see, are indicative of the mismatched perception within the entities they represent, of the disconnect inherent between who they believe themselves to be, who they aspire to be, and regrettably, who they will never become. This neverending dilemma is very reminiscent of the age-old combination rabbit-duck ambiguous drawing, as far as the brain's perception is initially concerned; usually, therefore, its reasoning is entrapped in an endless cycle of is it a rabbit-duck-rabbit-duck-rab--?

We, as entities, are ourselves collections of unique constellations of galaxies, which very well may never be in perfect alignment with one another (as far as interpretations of their reality go). These voids, therefore, are conceptually present because they do not understand, nor do they wish to understand, one another enough to arrive in cohesion. Voids of such hidden potential, indeed, you see, are thus rumored to contain multitudes of collected carbon echoes, and even the softest echo was not neglected when the voids did their sorting in time immemorial, with the greatest care indeed.

5. WISDOM OF MEMORY

Sometimes, I proclaim things wholly outside of who I think myself to be. It's often as though I'm my mother given visage and yet again breath, while at the same time, expected to behave as her even though I don't know who, actually, is my mother? Not in terms of question of parentage, no but deeper, What makes my mother who she is? It's enough to distract—nay, to fracture my concentration, my psyche, even my very memory to which I frequently cling like salvage in an ocean of uncertainty and pockets of unanswered, ceaseless questions. Despite all those tides of ambiguity, I am absolutely sure that what I proclaim stems from my mother's mouth. As a consequence of this bastion of certainty, I became for a time convinced that she and I would in fact be able to communicate clearly over the vastness that separates us.

In such occurrences of this state, my awareness expanded to include the foggy barrier in my brain that, lifted, connected me to such profound as-yet hidden discoveries deep within my memories—which sometimes indeed were not of my own making. In fact, these occasionally represented my ancestors and distant relatives, accessible whenever I might wish to entreat them for wisdom.

3. FIXED-POINT RUMINATIONS

I frequently ponder whether or not the mirror of which I am aware actually is operating from reflection of light; rather, possibly, than the reflection of reality as seen in an indeterminate multiverse, benevolently or malevolently granting me access when I happen to glance over at the silverback. As the innocuous mirror is forever leaving behind little benedictions of infant shadow clusters behind my eyes whenever I manage to disengage them from the surface, I remain unassuaged. However, to somewhat counteract this quixotic imbalance, I am sacrosanct in my belief that, within those potentialities that I behold through the dubious allowance of my curious reflection, I, in my cognizance of myself, am a fixed point, incontrovertible in all realities that reveal themselves to me thusly.

4. LEGIONS OF CREEPING DOOM

Every past already occurred, all potential futures yet to, and each inherently imperfect, flawed present, are with every piling and advancing certainty upon them declared: monstrous. They fill and infest every available kept space, relishing in the decadent freedom granted fully by each unfolding night cycle.

1. CERTIDUMBRE HECHIZADA

The convicted, utter certainty which I intermittently am hosting, therefore, may—I am understandably unmoored, so potentially, incorrect—progressively be hacked at and massacred tonight, as though it were the inaugural sacrificial bull of the French Revolution, its roasting putting alight a cache of societal, tinder-dry gunpowder just waiting—salivating potentially to combustion—for the signal to be given by their first martyr. However, in such a retribution not every soul will survive; rather of course will damnation be foisted upon those hallmarked by the Martyr's designated antebellum sign, serving their fervent lack of faith to dispatch them swiftly and unceremoniously.

This pain represented will be, in fact, throughout the entire affair the only constant universally applied to all souls; ultimately, it is the only data and determination within one's existence to make a substantive difference. Any residual doubt left behind after such a determination as final as that, therefore, must be present entirely because some external force has applied itself to, and is watching me, to such a degree as to unbalance the flawless scales of the exercise.

0 AND 1. WOULD YOU HAVE INSTEAD, A SIX?

An entity that is one may only become a dream, or a quill as an instrument to depict the realities of other potentials (?), or indeed become a day shot through with the most permeable heat. A zero, however, may manifest in complete contrast of flexibility and fully extant outside any temporal restriction or continuum. This is how my mind's consciousness manifests its active presence to me: entities may either become ones, or zeros. Upon doing so and effecting such a decision, they forfeit and consequently forget any prior time wherein they consisted of all possible numerical representations, and they cease to distinguish or signify this more and more with each day which may pass.

2. SELF-SUFFICIENCY IN SPITE, FLOURISHING

Those components which, collectively, represent myself across the many universes, long ago decided to summarily eschew the company of men, preferring the vastly more amenable growth proffered generously by comparison, instead through the sun.

6. BUTTERFLY

You would do well to consistently keep in mind the rippling effect that our kisses beset upon our ages and lives in general; for even as we exist at a typically advancing oscillating rate through time, the entire potentiality ofevery kiss we may ever share existed all at once: in that little breath of air first birthed before our lips met.

0. INEVITABILITY

You see, ultimately all remains in flux within this framework. Everything, at once, inherently chooses to be zero, at the same time it chooses to become one, then, the unfathomable as everything throws understanding into a singularity, instead choosing the heretofore forbidden both and neither. Complete subjectivity reigns wherever certainty has abdicated.

Close your eyes, so that I may suffuse myself in you, become your twin... I am you. We are everything. We are one, collectively, all while too we are zero. We become and are the time it takes for an electron to travel around and return to orbiting the nucleus of an atom of your skin.

This, therefore, is an inherent, unceasing time where I, you, we....do not exist.

Planck time.

THE SHAPES OF AIR
was composed with PT Sans and Advent Pro fonts.
The editing, layout and digital publishing
have been carried out by the author.
Osorno, Chile, 2022.

You are made of time.

Made in the USA
Coppell, TX
12 August 2022

81335523R00055